For Alice
JE

For a special dad.
We miss you very much xxx
RH

First published 2006 by Macmillan Children's Books
a division of Macmillan Publishers Limited
20 New Wharf Road, London N1 9RR
Basingstoke and Oxford
Associated companies throughout the world
www.panmacmillan.com

ISBN-13: 978-1-405-05190-3
ISBN-10: 1-405-05190-6

Printed in Belgium by Proost

This Way, Ruby!

Written by
Jonathan Emmett

Illustrated by
Rebecca Harry

MACMILLAN CHILDREN'S BOOKS

Once upon a time,
upon a nest,
beside a lake,
there lived a family of ducks.

A mother duck,

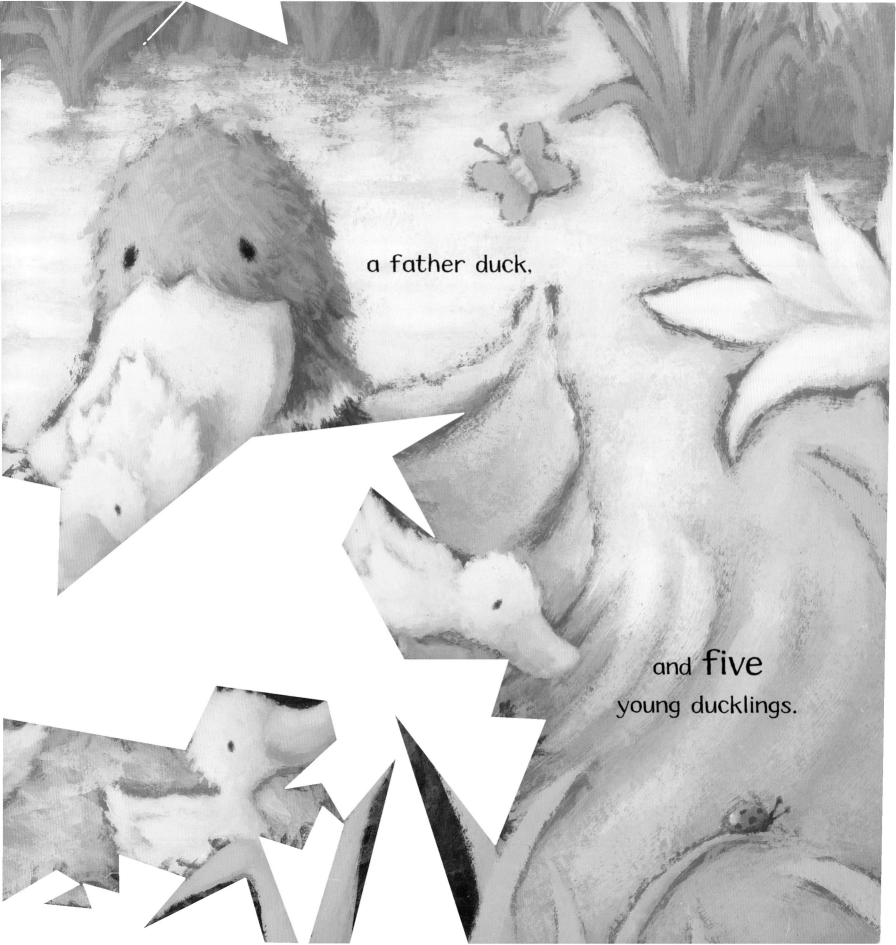

a father duck,

and **five** young ducklings.

Four of the ducklings were big and bold and were always rushing off in search of an adventure. Their names were

Rufus

Rory

Rosie

and Rebecca.

But the fifth duckling was small and steady
and took things slowly, in her own time.
And her name was RUBY.

It was a bright spring day and Mother Duck and Father Duck were snoozing in the sun.

"Let's go and explore," said Rufus, running down –

splash!

– into the water.

Rory, Rosie and Rebecca ran straight after him,
but Ruby stayed by the nest.

"This way, Ruby!"
called the others.

Ruby didn't want to be left behind,
so she swam after them.

Ruby caught up with them
at the edge of the reed beds.

Rufus, Rory, Rosie and Rebecca raced on
through a gap in the tall green stems.

But Ruby stopped to look around.
She saw a small waterfall that sparkled in the sun, and
a great golden fish that glimmered in the depths.

"Look!" said Ruby — but the
others did not stop.

"THIS WAY, RUBY!" they called.

Ruby joined the other ducklings in the middle of the reed beds.

Rufus, Rory, Rosie and Rebecca rushed off down a winding waterway.

But Ruby stopped to look around.
She saw the water lilies with their bright purple flowers,
and the four fat frogs that lay lazing on the leaves.

"Look!" said Ruby — but the
others did not stop.

"THIS WAY, RUBY!" they called.

Ruby found the other ducklings at the far side of the reed beds.

Rufus, Rory, Rosie and Rebecca ran straight up the grassy bank.

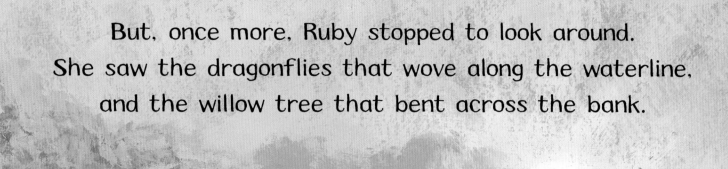

But, once more, Ruby stopped to look around.
She saw the dragonflies that wove along the waterline,
and the willow tree that bent across the bank.

AND she saw the
big black storm cloud that was
sweeping across the sky.

"Look!" said Ruby — but the
others did not stop.

"THIS WAY, RUBY!" they called.

Rufus, Rory, Rosie and Rebecca were rambling through the long grass when a flash of lightning lit the sky above them and a crash of thunder filled the air.

"THIS WAY!" they cried.
And they all ran off in different directions .
and then ran back again.

They were lost and they were scared and they wanted to go home — but they DIDN'T KNOW which way to go.

The ducklings huddled together anxiously
as something rustled through the grass . . .

It was RUBY!

Ruby was scared too – but
she DID KNOW which way to go!

She spotted the top of the willow tree
sticking up above the long grass.
"This way!" she called.

Ruby led the other ducklings down the bank and out onto the water.

Then she spotted the bright purple flowers floating among the reeds.

"This way!" she called.

Ruby arrived at the water lilies – and stopped.
The water wound off in many directions.
And they all looked the same.
She could not SEE which way to go.

"Which way, Ruby? WHICH WAY?" cried the other ducklings — as the big black storm cloud moved across the sun.

"Shush!" said Ruby. Then she swam around, slowly,
until she could just hear it — the gurgling
of the waterfall.

"This way!" she said, following the sound.

"Where have you been?" called Father Duck,
as the ducklings popped out of the reed beds.

"We had an adventure,"
panted Rufus.

"And we got lost!"
gasped Rory.

"But Ruby found us,"
added Rosie.

"And brought us home,"
Rebecca said.

"Well done, Ruby!" said Mother Duck proudly.
But Ruby had already gone.

The storm cloud had moved off, but Ruby felt
that they'd done enough exploring for one day.
It was time to go home.

"THIS WAY, EVERYONE!"
she called.